D0550920

SOPHIE AND THE
RESOURCE CENTRE
WESTERN ISLES LIBRARIES

Readers are requested to take great care of the item while in their possession, and to point out any defects that they may notice in them to the Librarian.
This item should be returned on or before the latest date stamped below, but an extension of the period of loan may be granted when desired.

DATE OF RETURN	DATE OF RETURN	DATE OF RETURN
Scalpay. 10/07		
Shawbost Oct 11		
Uig – Apr. 12		
Tolsta – Jul.12		
Uist.Bx3. Jul 14		
P1-3 Bar 1		

By the same author:

Sophie and the Albino Camel

Sophie
and the
LOCUST CURSE

STEPHEN DAVIES

ILLUSTRATED BY DAVE SHELTON

Ⓐ

ANDERSEN PRESS
LONDON

This book is dedicated to the
Fulani people of Burkino Faso:
Alla hokku jam

First published in 2007 by
Andersen Press Limited,
20 Vauxhall Bridge Road, London SWIV 2SA
www.andersenpress.co.uk

British Library Cataloguing in Publication Data available

ISBN 978 1 84270 625 1

Typeset by FiSH Books, Enfield, Middx.
Printed and bound in Great Britain by
Bookmarque Ltd., Croydon, Surrey

Chapter 1

'Good morning,' said Sophie's dad, wandering into the kitchen. 'Have you seen my motorbike goggles?'

'No,' said Sophie, who was standing on tiptoes searching in a wall cupboard. 'Have you seen the maize flakes?'

'I was wearing them when I came back from my research trip, but I can't for the life of me remember where I put them.'

Sophie's father was a botanist who had come to West Africa to research carnivorous plants. For three years now they had lived in a country called Burkina Faso in a small town called Gorom-Gorom.

Sophie put her cereal bowl back in the cupboard and picked up a mango. 'Dad,' she said, 'where's the fruit knife?'

'Never mess with knives,' said Sophie's father, leaving the room.

Sophie found the fruit knife and began to peel her mango. She worked quickly, knowing that her friend Gidaado could arrive any moment. When Sophie and her dad had first come to Burkina Faso three years ago she had found it very hard to fit in, but meeting Gidaado had made things easier. One friend her age was better than none.

Today was market day in Gorom-Gorom so there was no school, and Gidaado had invited Sophie to come to his village for the naming ceremony of his newborn cousin. Sophie had never been to a naming ceremony here and she was very excited.

Sophie cut her mango into bite-sized cubes and popped them into her mouth. On the kitchen table a radio was burbling away – a young woman reading the news in French, the official language of Burkina Faso. Sophie was not paying much attention to the news, but when she heard mention of their town Gorom-Gorom her ears pricked up.

'Gorom-Gorom is thought to be the next town under threat from *sauterelles*,' the newsreader was saying. 'Last night they wreaked havoc in Djibo and Aribinda and this morning they are moving east towards Gorom-Gorom. On our early morning show, "Wake up with Fatimata", General Alai Crêpe-Sombo criticised the government for its "slow and inadequate" response to the unfolding crisis...'

'Dad!' shouted Sophie. 'What are *sauterelles*?'

Her dad's voice from the study was faint. 'I already found them, thank you,' he said. 'They were in the *bath* of all places.'

Sophie sighed. Perhaps the *sauterelles* were djinns, mischievous spirits of the desert. Or perhaps they were monsters, half-man half-frog. After all, didn't the French word *sauter* mean 'jump'? Sophie went to the window and peered out, half expecting to see a horde of jumping djinns or slavering monsters pogo-ing towards the house. But all she saw were a few fire finches and her dad's sunflowers swaying in the breeze.

A sudden snort in the street outside made Sophie jump. A metal flap in the gate lifted up and a thin black hand came into view, fumbling with the bolt on the inside.

'Dad!' cried Sophie. 'Gidaado is here! Don't forget to pick me up from his village tonight, will you?'

'No thanks, dear,' came a faint voice from the study. 'I've had two cups already this morning.'

'*Salam alaykum*,' called Gidaado, leading his white camel in through the gate.

'*Alaykum asalam*,' said Sophie.

Gidaado was holding a long wooden staff and on his head he wore the traditional floppy cap of the griot clan. Griots were professional story-tellers and musicians. They knew thousands of stories, riddles and songs, and they were also experts in family history. Whenever there was an important party, a wedding or a naming ceremony, a griot or two would be invited to come and sing about the host's ancestors.

'Did you pass the night in peace?' said Sophie in Fulfulde, Gorom-Gorom's local language. Having lived here for three years she was fluent in Fulfulde, although she still spoke it with a slight English accent.

'Peace only,' said Gidaado. 'Did you wake in peace?'

'Peace only. How is Chobbal?'

'Peace only.' Gidaado stroked the snowy neck of the camel which knelt beside him. He had named the camel after his own favourite food, chobbal, a kind of millet porridge.

Sophie stepped up into the saddle on the camel's hump and rested her feet in the U of the neck. Gidaado jumped up behind her, raised his staff and clicked deep down in his throat. Chobbal's back legs unfolded, rocking the children forward, and then his front legs, lifting them high up into the air.

'Gidaado,' said Sophie as they moved off, 'what are *sauterelles*? It says on the radio that *sauterelles* are coming to Gorom-Gorom, but I don't know what the word means.'

'Don't ask me,' said Gidaado. 'That fire finch over there probably knows more French than I do.'

Sophie laughed. She knew that Gidaado did not go to school and that her question had been a long shot. Even though French was the official language of Burkina Faso, not many people spoke it. Here in Gorom-Gorom everyone used Fulfulde.

'Don't worry about it,' said Gidaado. 'I'm sure it's nothing interesting.'

Sophie was doubtful, but she tried to put it out of her mind. 'Are you ready for the naming ceremony?' she asked.

'Yes, of course,' said Gidaado. 'The baby is my cousin so when I do the *tarik* it's my own ancestors I'll be singing about. Couldn't be easier.'

'Are you singing on your own?' asked Sophie.

'Probably not – the other Giriiji griots should be there too.'

Chobbal the camel went out of the gate and walked up the street towards the market. His movement rocked the children on his hump gently backwards and forwards. A town crier was walking down the road ahead of them, banging his tam-tam and shouting at the top of his voice.

'RED SPECKLED COW!' yelled the town crier. 'LAST SEEN ON WEDNESDAY MORNING GRAZING NEAR TONDIAKARA! IF YOU KNOW WHERE SHE IS, CONTACT YUSUF DIKKO!'

Here in Gorom-Gorom Sophie heard criers almost every day. They announced naming ceremonies, weddings, funerals, and messages from the town authorities. If there was going to be a vaccination programme in town, a crier would let people know about it. If a serious crime was committed, a crier would go round appealing for information. But the most common job of a crier was to announce descriptions of missing cows. In Gorom-Gorom there were thousands of cows and every morning they would leave town and go out to the scrubland to graze. Every evening there were some which did not come home.

Gidaado was chuckling to himself. 'Hey, Sophie,' he said. 'What's the difference between a crier and a donkey?'

'I don't know.'

'Hit the donkey and he'll stop braying.'

Sophie did not laugh. 'He is only doing his job,' she said. 'Let's stop, Gidaado, I want to ask him what *sauterelles* are.'

'It's no good asking a crier something clever like that,' said Gidaado. 'He doesn't even know if it is morning or evening.'

Sophie scowled. What made griots so great that they could make fun of people doing other jobs?

'*Excusez-moi, monsieur*,' she said as they drew level with the crier. 'Do you speak French?'

The crier stopped banging his tam-tam and turned to look at her. 'Do I look like a schoolteacher?' he said in Fulfulde.

'No,' said Sophie.

'Or a schoolboy?'

'No,' said Sophie.

'Then what would I want with French?' said the crier.

'I don't know,' said Sophie, embarrassed. 'I just thought—'

The crier spread wide his arms. 'Did my grandfather and my father's grandfather speak French?'

'No,' said Sophie again. She could hear Gidaado chortling behind her, and elbowed him in the ribs to shut him up. 'Have you heard the news today?' she asked the crier.

'Yes. Yusuf Dikko has lost his red speckled cow, last seen on Wednesday grazing near—'

'No,' said Sophie. 'I mean really bad news. Like something dangerous on its way here.'

'I am a crier,' said the crier. 'I know about lost cows and found goats and new babies. If you want really bad news, go and listen to a radio.'

'I did,' said Sophie, 'but no one around here can tell me what it said.'

The crier scowled and moved on, beating his tam-tam. 'RED SPECKLED COW!' he yelled. 'LAST SEEN ON WEDNESDAY MORNING GRAZING NEAR TONDIAKARA! IF YOU KNOW WHERE SHE IS, CONTACT YUSUF DIKKO!'

'Thanks for your help,' muttered Sophie.

'Come on,' said Gidaado behind her, 'we're late for the ceremony. HOOSH-KA!' he yelled, twirling his staff in the air. Chobbal broke into a run and Sophie grabbed the wooden prongs on the front of the saddle just in time to avoid falling off.

'Gidaado!' shrieked Sophie. 'You know it is forbidden for animals to run in the market.'

'He's trotting, not running,' said Gidaado. 'HOOSH-BARAKAAAA!'

Chobbal picked up his hooves and the huts and stalls on either side became a blur. The rushing wind tousled Sophie's hair and blasted hotly against her eyeballs.

'*Now* he's running!' said Gidaado.

Chapter 2

Sophie screamed again. Galloping in the market was not like galloping in the desert. Not only was it forbidden, it was also terrifying. The streets of Gorom-Gorom's central market swarmed with men and women. When they heard the sound of hooves behind them, they turned round to find a white camel bearing down upon them. Children fled, cyclists swerved and old men jumped aside with remarkable agility.

Just in front of them strolled a young woman carrying a plate of fried fish on her head. The baby on her back was crying so loudly that she did not hear the approaching camel. Sophie closed her eyes and yanked the reins sharply to the right, sending Chobbal careering into a fruit stall. There was a yellow-green explosion as bananas, guavas and mangos scattered far and wide. Chobbal charged on through the debris and the stallholder jumped up and shook his fist at Sophie. '*A hanyan!*' he roared after her, which was not a polite thing to say.

Gidaado whooped. 'That was a near miss,' he yelled.

'You call that a *miss*?' said Sophie, wiping bits of over-ripe mango off her face.

As they neared the police post on the edge of town, a man in a smart khaki uniform stepped out into the road and waved at them to stop. Chobbal did not even break his stride.

'*Arrêtez!*' shouted the policeman, reaching for the pistol in his holster.

'Gidaado!' screamed Sophie.

Gidaado peered round Sophie and waved his staff cheerily at the policeman. 'UNCLE DEMBO!' he bellowed. 'WE'RE LATE FOR IBRAHIIM'S NAMING CEREMONY.'

The policeman's stern face broke into a grin of recognition. 'HURRY UP THEN, GIDA,' he shouted in Fulfulde, 'AND GIVE MY APOLOGIES TO IBRAHIIM! I AM ON DUTY ALL DAY!'

On the outskirts of Gorom-Gorom a mobile phone mast was being erected, the first one in the whole province. A crowd of curious children stood at a safe distance and watched open-mouthed as workmen heaved on the mast's tension cables.

The cattle market and the water tower flashed past and then the road came to an abrupt end. Chobbal galloped on eagerly into the sand. Looking back, Sophie saw the town's enormous welcome sign written in French and Fulfulde:

BIENVENUE À GOROM-GOROM!
GOROM-GOROM WI'I BISMILLAHI!

Welcome to Gorom-Gorom, read Sophie, and she thought again of the *sauterelles* which were at that very moment on their way here. *What could they be?* Gigantic carnivorous plants, perhaps. That would give her dad something to study. He was in his fourth year of research here and still had not found anything truly spectacular. But, thought Sophie, one of the *sauterelles* would probably eat Dad alive before he could even set up his microscope.

Gidaado's voice in Sophie's ear interrupted these morbid thoughts. 'See that big white rock?' he shouted, pointing with his staff.

'Yes,' yelled Sophie.

'That's Tondiakara, where the magicians go at night to sacrifice chickens.'

'Lovely!' said Sophie.

'And you see that tree with the big round fruit hanging from it?'

'Yes. It's a calabash tree, isn't it?'

'Not just any old calabash tree,' said Gidaado. 'That's the Sheik Amadou calabash tree. Sheik Amadou sits under that tree every day from sunrise to sunset, meditating on all the needless suffering in the world.'

'So how come he isn't sitting there now?'

'He's in hospital,' said Gidaado. 'A calabash fell on his head last Thursday.'

Sophie looked all around her at the desert. It was flat and featureless except for a few straggly thorn bushes. No *sauterelles* here yet, she thought. Unless they had excellent camouflage.

Chobbal let out a sudden snort of rage and began to buck up and down violently as he ran.

Sophie screamed. 'What's the matter with him?' she shouted. She twisted round in the saddle and saw immediately what the matter was. A tall boy was riding close behind them on a bicycle, gripping the handlebars with one hand and Chobbal's tail with the other.

'Let go of him, Saman!' Gidaado yelled.

'*Salam alaykum*, skink-teeth,' said the boy. 'Did you wake in peace? Where are you and your white girlfriend going this morning?'

'She's not my – *let GO*!' Gidaado leaned over and tried to prise the boy's hand off Chobbal's tail.

The boy hung on tight and laughed an idiotic high-pitched laugh. 'What a freaky camel,' he cried. 'Does he always jump up and down when he runs?'

'Gidaado,' whispered Sophie. 'Your staff.'

'Ah yes,' said Gidaado. He reached down as far as he could and inserted the end of his staff neatly between the spokes of the boy's front wheel. Sophie winced and closed her eyes.

'He's okay,' said Gidaado a moment later. 'The sand makes a nice soft landing.'

'Who is he?' asked Sophie.

'Sam Saman,' said Gidaado. 'He's one of the Gorom-Gorom griots.'

'He doesn't like you much, does he?'

14

'No,' said Gidaado. 'Saman and I go back a long way. We'd better watch our backs over the next few days, Sophie. Sam Saman is not the most forgiving griot in town.'

Sophie looked at her watch. 'Talking of griots,' she said, 'do you think the Giriiji griots will start the *tarik* without you? We're really late.'

Gidaado chuckled. 'Start the *tarik* without me?' he said. 'Can you start to make bricks without earth? Can you start to make chobbal without milk?'

'No.'

'There you are then. My role in the performance of the *tarik* is essential. The Giriiji griots would rather smash their *hoddus* over their own heads than start the *tarik* without me.'

A *hoddu* was a three-stringed guitar, used by griots to accompany their stories.

'I don't see why you are so indispensable,' said Sophie. 'I thought the *tarik* was just a list of names. Thig son of Thag, Thag son of Thog, and so on.'

'You know nothing about the *tarik*,' said Gidaado, piqued. 'The *tarik* is not just a list of names. The *tarik* is like the spine of a man, the roots of a tree, the water in which a fish swims.

When we are born we find it, when we die we become part of it. The *tarik* is the fabric of our life, a dazzling light shining down the well of History.'

'The well of History,' said Sophie. 'Ooooh, *deep*.'

'Mock if you like,' said Gidaado. 'You people know nothing about History. Even if History was to fall on your head like Sheik Amadou's calabash, you would not feel it. Even if History was bellowed in your ear by Furki Baa Turki, you would not hear it.'

Sophie had heard Furki Baa Turki bellow and she was certain that Gidaado was wrong. Furki Baa Turki was a town crier and he had the loudest voice of all the criers in the province. When he made announcements in Gorom-Gorom market, stallholders would plug their ears and beg for mercy. Besides, thought Sophie, how dare Gidaado talk like that. She sat and fumed silently.

Perched behind her, Gidaado was singing under his breath. He's practising the *tarik*, thought Sophie. I hope he forgets his lines in the middle of the ceremony.

Chobbal pounded onwards, rocking the children backwards and forwards on his hump.

The sun climbed higher and higher in the sky until the sand of the desert glared like an overexposed photograph. After a long while Sophie reached into her shoulder bag and took out her water bottle and a small tub of sun-cream. Gidaado reached round her and took Chobbal's reins from Sophie so that she could smear the cream on her face and arms.

'Are you still mad at me?' he asked.

'Yes,' she replied, hiding a smile.

It was eleven o'clock by the time the children reached the fields of Giriiji, Gidaado's village. Here the villagers' crops stood tall and proud, thousands of millet plants, each plant bearing its precious cargo of crisp golden grains. Harvest time was not far away.

At last they arrived at a small group of mud-brick huts. Next to one of these huts the men and women of Giriiji were sitting on straw mats in the shade of a large acacia tree. Sophie heard the clacking of calabashes.

'I don't believe it,' said Gidaado.

'What?'

'They've started the *tarik* without me,' said Gidaado.

Chapter 3

'*BAHAAT-UGH!!*' cried Sophie, camel-language for *stop*.

Chobbal skidded to a halt and Gidaado sprang off the hump backwards. He landed in a heap on the ground, got up, brushed himself down and ran over to the musicians' mat where his three-stringed guitar was waiting for him. Sophie dismounted more carefully and went to join the spectators.

'Amidou my brother, same father, same mother, flesh of my own flesh,' sang the lead musician. Sophie recognized him as Gidaado's

Uncle Ibrahiim, the leader of the Giriiji griots. He was flanked by Gidaado's cousins Hassan and Hussein, who were bashing away happily on a pair of calabashes. Gidaado sat down behind them and began to pluck his *hoddu*.

'Amidou, husband of Bintu the Beautiful, brother of Alu the Fearless,' sang Uncle Ibrahiim. 'Alu the Fearless who wrestled a lion and did lots of other brave and brainless things.'

'That's right!' shouted Gidaado.

Sophie noticed Gidaado's grandmother sitting on one of the women's mats. She had great long earlobes and her skin was as wrinkly as a wal-nut. Her eyes were half-closed and she nodded to the calabash beat.

'Amidou and Alu, sons of Hamadou, son of Yero the son of Tijani,' sang Ibrahiim.

'That's right!' shouted Gidaado.

'Tijani, whose camel Mad Mariama ran faster than the harmattan wind.'

'That's right!'

It seemed to Sophie that Gidaado's role in the *tarik* was slightly less glamorous than he had made out. Perhaps the best was yet to come.

'Tijani son of Haroun.'

'That's right!'

19

'Husband of Halimatu the Horrible, who could make music with her armpits.'

'That's right!'

'Son of Salif, son of Ali, son of Gorko Bobo.'

'That's ri—'

'STOP!' shouted the chief.

Uncle Ibrahiim stopped singing and blinked rapidly as if waking from a trance. The twins' calabashes ceased their clicking and clacking. Gidaado laid down his *hoddu* and stared at the chief in amazement. A woman emerged from the nearest mud-brick hut, holding a tiny baby at her breast. She quivered with rage and pointed a long thin forefinger at the chief.

'How dare you interrupt the *tarik*, you son of a skink!' she cried.

The villagers gasped. A skink was a large lizard and not a nice thing to call anybody, let alone a village chief.

'Bintu,' hissed a nervous-looking man in the front row of the audience. 'Bintu, don't talk like that.'

'How am I supposed to talk? He has shattered the *tarik* and brought shame on the memory of all our ancestors.'

The villagers gasped again. This was a

serious accusation. All eyes now were on Al Hajji Diallo, chief of Giriiji.

Slowly the chief raised his eyes to heaven. 'Look!' he cried.

Everyone looked. Far away in the west, a pink cloud was gathering in the sky, thickening and getting closer, like a dust cloud. Here in the desert a dust cloud was usually good news, indicating the arrival of rain.

'*Zorki*,' said Uncle Ibrahiim.

This was no dust cloud. As it approached, Sophie could see that the cloud was made up of millions of tiny dots, pink and flickering and strangely beautiful.

'*Zorki*,' said the woman with the baby.

'What is it?' asked Gidaado's grandmother loudly. 'Why has the *tarik* stopped? What is going on?'

'The pink death,' said the chief. 'The pink death is coming!'

'*Zorki*!' shrieked Gidaado's grandmother.

The dots swarmed towards the fields and began to dive. They fell like rain, no longer dots but living creatures now. The air was thick with legs and wings and mandibles. So these are the *sauterelles*, thought Sophie. *Locusts*.

*

In no time at all Sophie found herself sprinting through the millet plants alongside Gidaado. She glanced down guiltily at the long curved scythe in her hands. *Never mess with knives*, her dad was always saying. If he could see her now his glasses would steam up and he would no doubt give her that lecture about Hibata Zan running to school holding a pair of scissors. She wore an eye-patch to this day, poor girl.

'Gidaado,' said Sophie as they ran. 'Why do they call it the "pink death"?'

'Well,' said Gidaado. 'The locusts are pink. And by eating the harvest they bring – you know.'

'I see.'

Arriving at Gidaado's field, Sophie handed Gidaado one of the scythes and he quickly showed her how to harvest the millet. Stalk in your left hand, scythe in your right hand and *slice*. 'Now you try,' he said.

Slice, slice, slice, went the two scythes, and the millet stalks fell this way and that. On every side Sophie heard the slice and crunch of other harvesters. All the people of Giriiji, young and old, were working together to save the millet. After all, this was their food for the coming year.

A locust landed on a stalk right in front of Sophie, hugged the millet with its jointed legs and started munching. Another flew in Sophie's face; she screamed and batted it away. She sliced the stalk with her scythe but immediately two more locusts landed on it. Sophie dropped the stalk and stamped on them. *Crunch. Crunch.*

The insects were all around her now, chomping and chattering. They were on her clothes and in her hair. There was not a single head of millet that did not have two, three, four locusts clinging to it, even the harvested millet lying on the ground. Sophie watched the locusts devour Giriiji's millet crop and she blinked hard to stop herself bursting into tears.

Chapter 4

The shadows of day were lengthening and fading and the sun gradually turned the colour of blood. Underneath the acacia tree, the people of Giriiji took their places on the same straw mats that they had abandoned in such a hurry that morning. All around them the millet plants stood like a conquered army, a million headless stalks bearing witness to the day's disastrous battle.

The villagers had done their best to save the harvest and they had lost. The locusts had gobbled every last grain of millet in the fields and launched smugly into the sky, heading south to wreak more devastation.

The people of Giriiji now sat dazed and exhausted, gazing at the setting sun. Seated cross-legged on the children's mat, Sophie watched the edge of the red orb kiss the horizon and dip out of sight.

Al Hajji Diallo sat in his wicker chair surrounded by the village elders, and in the gathering dusk he looked old and frail. He cleared his throat and began to speak in a low even voice.

'The Lord gives,' he said, 'and the Lord takes away. Blessed be the name of the Lord.'

There was a long silence. A red-necked lizard scuttled up to Sophie, bobbed up and down as if it was doing press-ups, then scuttled off again. No one spoke.

'Blessed be the name of the Lord,' repeated the chief. 'He knows why these things happen.'

There was a quiet 'amen' from one of the elders.

'Today,' continued the chief, 'we are celebrating the birth of Mariama, daughter to Amidou and Bintu. Now that the sun has set, let the dancing begin.'

Sophie could not believe that they intended to go ahead with the dancing after what had happened. Never in her life had she felt less like dancing.

Uncle Ibrahiim walked forward slowly, took off his sandals and stepped onto the musicians' mat. He knelt down, positioned his *hoddu* and began to play.

Ibrahiim's music was melodious and mystical and it was a tune that Sophie knew well. Gidaado had played this song for her once before and she had been unable to get it out of her head ever since.

> *'The desert rejoices and I with it,*
> *Praise to the Creator.'*

The villagers sat motionless on the straw mats and listened. Sophie thought of how happy she had been when she had got up this morning. She had been so excited about the prospect of spending the day at Gidaado's village and attending the naming ceremony. She had been singing this very song while she brushed her teeth, and had inadvertently sprayed toothpaste all over the mirror.

> *'The desert rejoices and I with it,*
> *Praise to the Creator.'*

The moon was rising now and cast a faint glow over the landscape. Without a word Gidaado's grandmother got up off her mat, hobbled to the front and began to dance. She shuffled from side to side, swinging her arms gently to the music and humming to herself. Another elderly woman went up and joined her. Ignoring their audience, they shuffled and swayed, smiling as if at some private joke.

'The desert dances and I with it,
Praise to the Creator.'

One by one the villagers got up and began to dance among their ravaged crops. Sophie desperately wanted to join in but she felt heavy with the pain and disappointment of the day. Maybe tomorrow or the next day she would dance, but not tonight.

Gidaado came out of nowhere and sat down beside her and in silence they watched the men and women of Giriiji moving in the moonlight. Finally, Gidaado spoke:

'Sophie, you know how it is when you are sitting close to the fire at night and tiny sparks jump out and make little scorch-marks on your feet and legs?'

'Yes,' said Sophie.

'We griots say that those sparks are like Suffering.'

'Whatever.'

'And you know how it is when you are milking a cow and tiny droplets of milk splash up out of the calabash and wet your face and arms?'

'No,' said Sophie.

'Well they do. We say that those droplets are like Joy.'

'And?'

'And nothing,' said Gidaado. 'Life is a mixture of the two, that's all. Sparks and droplets. Suffering and Joy.'

'You go and dance if you like,' said Sophie. 'I want to be on my own.'

It was gone nine o'clock when Sophie's dad arrived on the Yamaha to pick her up. His eyes behind his motorbike goggles were large and troubled.

'Sorry I'm late, darling,' he said breathlessly. 'Are you okay?'

'I'm okay,' said Sophie, taking her place behind him on the motorbike. 'But the millet isn't.'

28

'They arrived in Gorom-Gorom, too. I had *sauterelles* splatting on my goggles all the way here.'

'You know what the villagers call it?' said Sophie. 'The pink death.'

Her dad nodded and held up a small screw-topped jar. Inside the jar stood a single locust, tapping its front legs feebly against the glass as if pleading to be let out. 'I'm going to feed him to my desert flytrap,' said her dad, 'and see how long she takes to digest him.'

'Good idea,' said Sophie.

Her dad kicked down savagely on the starter and the motorbike roared into life. Sophie put her arms around his waist as he opened up the throttle and sped off into the night. On the dashboard a tiny GPS blinked at them, pointing the way home to Gorom-Gorom.

As they rode, the Yamaha's headlamp shone along the white sand and across occasional acacia bushes, and Sophie noticed that the passing swarm had stripped even the acacias of their leaves. She could not help thinking of Gidaado and his grandmother. They would have no millet in their grain store this year. How on earth would they survive?

Chapter 5

Sophie did not see Gidaado again for several days. She tried to concentrate on her school-work but none of it seemed important any more. The pink death had destroyed all the fields around Gorom-Gorom and an atmosphere of quiet despair hung over the town. The price of a sack of millet in the market had more than doubled since the locust invasion and everyone was finding it hard to buy food. Everyone except Sophie and her dad.

Early on market day, Sophie was just finishing her maize flakes when she heard a loud *'Bahaat-ugh!'* outside. She looked out of the window and there in the front yard knelt Chobbal. Gidaado slid off the camel's back and patted him fondly. 'I know you're hungry,' he said, 'but please don't eat Mr Brown's sunflowers.' Sophie went to the door to meet him.

'Salam alaykum, Gidaado!'

'Alaykum asalam, Sophie. Did you wake in peace?'

'Peace only, thank you. How is your village?'

'Peace only. There are no problems.'

Sophie knew this was not true – after all, there was a famine brewing in Giriiji. But when you greeted someone in Fulfulde it was important to pretend that everything was all right.

'How is your grandmother?'

'Peace only. How is your father?'

'Peace only. He is in the study, fiddling with his flytrap.'

'May God give peace.'

'Amen. Come on through to my room.'

Gidaado followed Sophie into her bedroom and they sat down. The room was rather bare compared to her bedroom back home, but it was comfortable. There was a mosquito net hanging

31

over her bed, a wooden desk, and a shelf for her schoolbooks.

'How are you, Gidaado?'

'Peace only. I have lost my job.'

'What do you mean?'

'My uncle has thrown me out of his music group. He says he needs me to get a different job so that we can earn enough to live on.'

Sophie considered this. Uncle Ibrahiim was probably right. If he and Gidaado worked separately rather than together then they could earn twice as much.

'Who will replace you in your uncle's music group?'

'Hassan, probably. And Hussein will play calabash on his own.'

'It won't be as good without you in it,' said Sophie.

'You haven't heard the worst bit,' said Gidaado. 'Guess what my uncle wants me to do for a job.'

'Sell fish?'

'Worse.'

'Wrestle lions?'

'Worse.'

'I give up.'

'He wants me to work as a crier.'

'That's not so bad, is it?' said Sophie. 'I think you'd make a good crier.'

Gidaado snorted. 'Sophie, you still seem to think that a griot and a crier are more or less the same thing. Well, they aren't. They're as different as stallion and skink.'

Not this again, thought Sophie.

'A griot is an artist,' said Gidaado, standing up. 'A griot crafts words that grab you by the intestines and swing you around. He soars in song above the desert eagle and straddles in speech vast oceans of wisdom. If a griot sings the "Ballad of Safietu and Pullori", the weeping in his village lasts for seven days. If he recites the conquests of Ousmana Dan Fodio, the cows are woken from their sleep by the sound of infidel knees a-knocking. If he tells the stories of the Ten Plagues of Egypt or the Omniscient Twins of Timbuktu, princes clutch his robes and beg for more.'

'And a crier?' said Sophie.

'A crier just stomps around town shouting his head off.'

Sophie shook her head. 'I think being a crier is a nice job,' she said.

'Right,' said Gidaado. 'I expect you think cleaning out the camel-pen at the market is a nice job, too. But that's because all you have ever done in your life is go to school and sit at a desk and—'

Gidaado broke off, staring wide-eyed at Sophie's bookshelf.

'What are *they*?' he asked, pointing.

On the bookshelf, next to Sophie's school-books stood three plastic flowers, yellow, orange and red. They all wore dark glasses and had big cheesy grins.

'They aren't real,' said Sophie. 'They are dancing flowers.'

'You're joking,' said Gidaado.

Sophie reached for her cassette box, and picked out 'Greatest Hits of Ali Farka Touré'. He was a singer from Mali who Gidaado had recommended to her, and his songs were a combination of traditional griot music and American blues. Sophie loved this album and always put it on when she felt down.

Sophie switched on her cassette player and inserted the cassette. She had asked her father for an ipod last Christmas, but he had refused. 'Where will you go to download songs?' Dad had said. 'You won't find mp3s in the desert,' he had said. 'Don't look at me like that,' he had said, 'there's nothing wrong with cassettes.'

Sophie jabbed PLAY and a lone African voice broke the silence with one long drawn-out note. It was the voice of Ali Farka Touré. The plastic flowers began to sway from side to side. Then came the familiar *clickety-clack* of ringed fingers on a calabash and a chorus of female voices; the flowers nodded and swayed in response. Gidaado watched them, his cheeks slack with wonder.

'How do they—?'

'Batteries,' said Sophie.

'The world is bitter,' sang the male voice in Fulfulde.

'The world is sweet,' sang the female chorus. Fading in underneath the singers was the patter of conga drums and the hauntingly beautiful moan of the slide guitar.

'That's Ali's brother Omar Farka Touré on the conga drums,' said Gidaado. 'And that's his cousin on the guitar.'

'I know,' said Sophie.

'I bet Ali Farka Touré never chucked *his* family out of his music group,' said Gidaado. 'I bet he never told *Omar* to go and get a job as a crier.'

'Be quiet,' said Sophie. 'We're coming to the good bit.'

The singers stopped abruptly and the calabash and conga drums grew faster and louder, beating out a joyful and infectious rhythm. The dancing flowers danced. What with their sunglasses and cheesy grins, the overall effect was hilarious. Gidaado let out a sudden snort of laughter and Sophie fell backwards on the bed giggling helplessly.

'Guess what I call them,' said Sophie through tears of laughter.

'What?'

'Salif, Ali and Gorko Bobo.'

'By giving them those names you have brought shame on all my ancestors,' said Gidaado in a shrill voice.

'I guess so,' said Sophie.

Gidaado scowled at her in mock fury and they burst out laughing again.

'I need to get going,' said Gidaado, wiping his eyes. 'Idrissa Gorel has lost his cow and he asked me to announce it in the animal market today.'

'All right.' Sophie pressed STOP and the dancing flowers slumped.

'Wish me luck,' said Gidaado as he left the room. 'If this doesn't work, me and my grandmother are dead.'

'Don't exaggerate,' called Sophie after him, but there was a lump in her throat as she said it.

Chapter 6

The animal market was a long walk from Sophie's house, situated on the north side of Gorom-Gorom. By the time Sophie arrived, the heat of the day had passed and there was even a breath of wind. She greeted the guardian at the market gate and slipped into the throng of buyers, sellers and gossipers.

The animal market was a large enclosure with different areas reserved for different kinds of animals. Sophie stood right in the middle of the enclosure; there were cattle in front of her, camels behind her, sheep and goats to her left and donkeys to her right. All around her milled a chattering squabbling bargaining mass of human beings. Some she recognized as townspeople but most were herders from far-flung villages like Giriiji, Yengerento and Bidi. Sophie headed for the cows.

It was usually possible to tell the buyers from the sellers. Buyers wandered around in fine long robes and surveyed the animals with beady, calculating eyes. Sellers wore simpler clothes and stood in nervous clusters, leaning on their staffs and pretending not to watch the buyers. A third group, the gossipers, were just there for a natter.

Normally, the Gorom-Gorom animal market was a fun place to be. After all, this was the social capital of the whole province, a place to catch up with friends and gaze at beautiful, long-horned cows. But today, the atmosphere was heavy. All around her Sophie heard the words 'pink death' repeated over and over in the solemn tone of voice you hear at funerals. The locusts seemed to be the sole topic of conversation at the animal market today.

'They came to Yengerento on Wednesday afternoon,' a herder near Sophie was saying. 'They were like a terrible army.'

'Yes,' said his companion. 'Locusts show no mercy.'

'They sent Abdullai Bodeejo insane, you know. We had to tie him up.'

'There has never been a worse harvest,' said another. 'Not since the Great Famine of 1972.'

'May God help us,' said another.

'BROWN ZEBU COW!' bellowed a voice behind the herders. 'LAST SEEN ON MONDAY BY THE JAWJAW BAOBAB TREE! CONTACT IDRISSA GOREL!'

Sophie recognized the voice. She ducked through the crowd and there before her stood Gidaado the Fourth.

'*Salam alaykum*,' she said.

'BROWN ZEBU COW!' Gidaado bellowed in her ear. 'HAVE YOU SEEN HER?'

'No, I have not,' said Sophie rubbing her ear. 'And I'm surprised you haven't got yourself arrested yet.'

'This is the stupidest job ever,' said Gidaado. 'Ten years of training in the griot art and what do I end up doing? Yelling about a brown zebu cow.'

Sophie was about to reply when Gidaado grabbed her arm and took off through the crowd, pulling her behind him. He dodged behind a herd of wide black bulls and crouched down.

'Who are we hiding from?' said Sophie.

'Sam Saman,' said Gidaado. 'I just saw him coming towards us.'

'Is he still mad about the other day?' said Sophie. She couldn't help smiling whenever she thought of the staff-in-the-spokes gag.

'No,' said Gidaado. 'He's delighted just to see me working as a crier. He has been following me around all day, crowing. Keeps on asking me if I am enjoying my new job.'

'Look on the bright side,' said Sophie. 'You get paid for this announcement.'

'Only if the cow is found.'

Sophie frowned. That was simply not fair.

'I'll tell you the real bright side,' continued Gidaado. 'At least my father isn't here to see his son working as a crier.'

Sophie looked away. She knew that Gidaado's father Alu the Fearless had died when Gidaado was about seven. Then she thought of her own mother. It had been a long time since she had died but still Sophie missed her.

'Look out!' shouted Gidaado.

There was a commotion amongst the cattle. A

frightened bull had broken away from its group and was careering through the crowd, bellowing in rage. People were squealing and running away, except for one brave young herder who dived onto the animal's tail and hung on there as it bucked furiously. Two other herders ran in to help; one of them slipped a noose of rope round the bull's back right leg, and tugged. The other tried to grab a front leg, leaping back and forth to evade the lunging horns.

The frenzied animal was too strong. It pulled the rope out of the herder's hands and started to charge again, dragging the younger man behind him. Sophie screamed – the bull was coming straight at her. *Fifteen metres, ten metres, five metres*. A tall thin man with a gun stepped briskly in front of Sophie, took aim and shot. The animal staggered and crashed to the ground at her feet. A cloud of red dust rose into the air.

'NO!' screamed Sophie. 'What have you done?'

Gidaado took hold of her arm. 'It's all right,' he said. 'That's a sleep gun. It fires a dart to make the bull go to sleep.'

Sophie felt very foolish. She knew all about

tranquillizer guns but she had not expected to see one here in Gorom-Gorom.

'Does that happen often?' she asked.

'Yes,' said Gidaado. 'With so many animals and people packed in together, it's not surprising some of them get frightened. It's always good if someone at the market has a sleep gun at the ready.'

Sophie took a deep breath to calm herself, and tried to remember what they had been talking about before the bull interrupted.

'That thing you said about being glad your father wasn't here to see you,' she said. 'You didn't mean that, did you?'

'I certainly did,' said Gidaado. 'It is shameful for a griot to work as a crier.'

'But you are doing it to support your family, Gidaado.'

'Supporting them and shaming them at the same time. Marvellous.'

Sophie thought again of her mother. What was it she used to say? *Whatever you find yourself doing, Sophie, do it as well as you can. Do it with all your heart and strength.*

'You are a crier now,' said Sophie bluntly. 'Try being a good one.'

Gidaado looked at Sophie as if seeing her for the first time. 'Boil your head,' he said, and walked off.

Chapter 7

For a whole week Sophie did not see Gidaado at all. She did not know if he had gone back to his village or if he was staying somewhere in Gorom-Gorom. But early on market day, while she was pouring her maize flakes, Sophie heard his familiar '*Bahaat-ugh!*' outside the window. She opened the front door and went outside.

'*Salam alaykum,*' said Gidaado, sliding off Chobbal's back. Sophie looked at him. Was it just her imagination or was Gidaado getting thinner?

'*Alaykum asalam,*' she said. 'Did you wake in peace?'

'Peace only. How is your father?'

'Peace only. How is your grandmother?'

'Peace only. She is angry with me because I have no money to buy her medicine this week.'

'That's not your fault,' said Sophie.

Gidaado shuffled his feet. 'Try telling her that,' he said.

'What about Uncle Ibrahiim?' asked Sophie. 'Can't he help?'

'My uncle's music group is not getting any work these days. Since the pink death came, people in Gorom have stopped inviting griots to their ceremonies. They are saying that the *tarik* is an unnecessary expense. How can they call the *tarik* "unnecessary"? If we stop singing the *tarik* at our naming ceremonies we might as well all be dead.'

Sophie did not know what to say. There was a long silence and she was relieved when Gidaado spoke again.

'Sophie,' he said. 'I'm sorry I told you to boil your head.'

'That's okay,' said Sophie.

'I'm glad you didn't boil your head,' continued Gidaado, 'because I need your help with something. I need a few words of French.'

'What do you want to say?'

'I want to say: "Have you seen my cow?"'

Sophie thought for a moment. Was it *mon vache* or *ma vache*? Probably *ma*. *'Est-ce que tu as vu ma vache?'* she said.

'Est-ce que tu as vu ma vache?' repeated Gidaado.

'Good.'

Gidaado turned and climbed back onto Chobbal's hump. 'One more thing,' he said. 'Can I borrow Salif, Ali and Gorko Bobo?'

'Sure.'

'I thought about what you said,' said Gidaado, crossing his feet in the U of Chobbal's neck. 'You may be pleased to know that today I plan to be the best crier Gorom-Gorom has ever seen.'

'Great,' said Sophie and she ran inside to fetch the dancing flowers.

When Sophie went to the animal market that afternoon, it did not take her long to find Gidaado. He was squatting on a straw mat in the middle of the marketplace. Behind him knelt Chobbal the albino camel, beside him stood the dancing flowers, and all around him stood a large crowd of herders and townspeople. Sophie was pleased to see that Gidaado was holding his *hoddu*.

'FIVE-YEAR-OLD COW, BROWN FACE, WHITE BODY, BIG UDDERS!' Gidaado was shouting. 'LAST SEEN HERE IN GOROM-GOROM. CONTACT BELKO SAMBO!'

'That's me,' said a wizened shepherd in the front row, turning and waving shyly to the crowd.

Gidaado stood his *hoddu* upright beside him on the mat and he started to pluck the strings, a complicated tune smattered with trills and grace notes. The dancing flowers began to boogy and the crowd chortled and pointed and tapped their feet to the music. Gidaado took a deep breath so that his whole body seemed to swell up, and then he began to sing:

> 'No milk since Tuesday,
> I wish I could die,
> My coffee is black
> And my chobbal is dry.
>
> *Bring back,*
> *Bring back,*
> *Oh, bring back Big Udders to me.*
> No milk since Tuesday
> And that's no mistake,
> I'm all of a twitter,
> I'm thin as a rake.

Bring back,
Bring back,
Oh, bring back Big Udders to me.

No milk since Tuesday,
I hate to complain,
But Beastlé milk powder
Just isn't the same.

Bring back,
Bring back,
Oh, bring back Big Udders
to meeeeeeeeeee.'

Gidaado gave three loud staccato taps on the body of the *hoddu* and beamed around at his audience. 'FIVE-YEAR-OLD COW, BROWN FACE, WHITE BODY, BIG UDDERS!' he yelled. 'LAST SEEN HERE IN GOROM-GOROM. CONTACT BELKO SAMBO!'

'I've seen that cow!' cried a young boy excitedly. 'It's in Bidi now. Mariama the marabout's wife is looking after it.'

'Praise the Lord!' shouted Belko Sambo pushing his way through the crowd towards the boy.

'Result,' said Gidaado, re-tuning his *hoddu*.

'And so to my next song. Imagine, if you will, a skinny-legged Zebu cow belonging to a certain Jibi Sisse. Yellow with red splotches. Last seen near Djinn Rock east of Aribinda. This is a very sophisticated song and one line of the chorus is even in French. Special thanks to my friend Sophie Brown for her help with the translation.'

Sophie tried not to blush and failed. Gidaado started plucking the strings again, swelled up and began to sing:

'My skinny-legged cow is astray in the bush
She is yellow with splotches of red.
If I don't find her soon she will hunger and thirst
And the djinns will jump on her head.

Has anybody seen my Skinny Legs?
Est-ce que tu as vu ma vache?
If you give me a hand to find Skinny Legs
I'll give you a bundle of cash.

For seven long days have I wandered the land
And listened for Skinny Legs' "Moo",
But all I have seen is her prints in the sand
And all I have smelled is her—'

'Excuse me, Mr Crier,' said a man at the back of the crowd, raising his hand timidly. 'Do you have any cassettes of your music for sale?'

Gidaado stared at him. 'Of course not,' he said. 'I'm not *that* good. Now where was I?' He swelled up and opened his mouth to sing again.

'Excuse me, Mr Crier,' said Sophie, thinking quickly. 'Do you think you could possibly record a cassette and make a few copies in time for next week's market?'

Gidaado looked at her. She winked meaningfully at him and nodded her head vigorously. *Say yes. Say yes. Say yes.*

Gidaado stared back blankly for a while and then a slow smile spread across his face. 'All right,' he said. 'Why not?'

Chapter 8

The recording sessions took longer than Sophie had expected. Gidaado was fine in practice but whenever she put the microphone in front of his mouth and pressed RECORD he got flustered and fluffed his lines. Eventually though they managed to record near-perfect versions of ten lost cow songs.

Sophie enjoyed designing the cassette covers. On each one she drew a picture of a cow's head, complete with boggly eyes and dangly tongue. Above the cow she wrote in bubble letters 'Greatest Hits Of Gidaado The Griot'. On the back she drew a copyright symbol and wrote out the titles of the songs in her best handwriting:

1. Lost under African skies
2. Where now Brown Cow?
3. Has anybody seen my Skinny Legs?
4. Losing You
5. Since my Daisy left me
6. Absent without leaves
7. Mucky Tail I miss you
8. No milk since Tuesday
9. Still haven't found what I'm looking for
10. Zebu Blues

Gidaado begged Sophie to let him record a bonus track ('Sam Saman Has A Face Like A Skink') but she refused, on the grounds that it was not in keeping with the rest of the album.

Gidaado was delighted when he saw the finished cassettes. 'You know, Sophie,' he said, 'as I have always said, working as a crier isn't all that bad.'

'Right,' smiled Sophie.

'Did you see Belko Sambo's face when he heard that Big Udders had been found? He was ecstatic.'

'Yes,' said Sophie. 'My dad looked like that when he found his first desert flytrap.'

'Of course,' said Gidaado. 'I'll have to practise a lot before I can shout as loud as Furki Baa Turki.' He took a deep breath.

Sophie chuckled and put her fingers in her ears.

On market day Gidaado turned up early at Sophie's house and they discussed where to set up Gidaado's stall.

'We can use Salif dan Bari's stall,' said Sophie. 'He got bitten by a rope in his field the other day and he's still at the clinic recovering.'

No one here called a snake a snake. People thought that if you said the word 'snake', the nearest snake would think you were calling it and would come looking for you. So they always said 'rope' instead.

When the children arrived at the market they found sure enough that the rope charmer's stall was empty. Gidaado took the tray of cassettes off his head and laid it carefully on the wooden trestle table. Sophie arranged the dancing flowers on one side and the cassette player on the other. Then she inserted a cassette and pressed PLAY.

'Oh no,' said Gidaado. 'Look who's coming.'

Sam Saman strolled up to the stall.

'*Salam alaykum*,' he said.

Gidaado did not answer. He gazed over the boy's shoulder as if something had caught his interest there.

'*Alaykum asalam*,' said Sophie.

'Gidaado, you're looking thin,' said Saman. 'Anyone would think you had not been eating.'

Gidaado glared at his rival and his hand closed into a tight fist.

'Don't,' whispered Sophie. 'If you start a fight, we'll be thrown out of the market. We can't afford that.'

Saman took one of the cassettes out of the tray and sneered at the picture on the front. 'Funny looking goat,' he said.

'It's a cow,' said Sophie.

'Greatest Hits of Gidaado the Griot,' read Saman. 'That should be "Gidaado the Crier", shouldn't it?'

Sophie reached over and turned up the volume on her cassette player as far as it would go.

'LOST UNDER AFRICAN SKIES!!!!' Gidaado's voice bellowed from the speakers and the dancing flowers went so wild that it seemed their stalks would break. Saman was still talking but Sophie and Gidaado could not hear a word; they just grinned at him while his mouth opened and closed like a fish. Saman soon got fed up and went on his way.

Gidaado turned the volume back down. 'Now do you wish we'd recorded that bonus track?' he said.

'Yes,' said Sophie.

Loud noise in the market always attracted a crowd, and soon there was a big audience huddled around Gidaado's stall, listening to the lost cow songs.

'Sophie,' said Gidaado out of the side of his mouth. 'How many of these cassettes do we have to sell?'

Sophie looked at her notebook. 'Well,' she whispered, 'if we sell two cassettes, we can buy your grandmother's medicine. If we sell five, that's a whole sack of millet.'

'What about if we sell all fifty?' said Gidaado. 'Can I buy a mobile phone?'

'Definitely,' grinned Sophie.

The crowd seemed to be enjoying the cassette. By the time they reached the chorus of 'Where Now Brown Cow?' several of the audience were chuckling and others were clapping in time. 'Has anybody seen my Skinny Legs?' went down even better. One poor lad laughed so hard he wet himself.

'A thousand francs for a cassette,' said Gidaado, when the last mournful chord of 'Zebu Blues' had died away. The audience stared back at him and one by one they shuffled off. One man began to count out small change in his palm but then he shook his head and left.

'Why aren't they buying?' said Sophie.

'I don't know,' said Gidaado. 'I suppose a thousand francs seems a lot when there is no millet in your grain store.'

Everybody had left except for one smartly-dressed black girl carrying a camel-skin handbag. Her hair was dyed dark red and it was arranged in dozens of intricate plaits. She's pretty, thought Sophie. And that hairdo alone must have cost a thousand francs.

'*Excusez-moi, monsieur,*' said the girl to Gidaado. '*J'aime bien votre cassette.*'

Gidaado simpered and nodded. He obviously did not understand a word.

'I'll handle this,' Sophie said to him in Fulfulde, and she turned to the red-haired girl. '*Comment t'appelles tu?*' she said in French. 'What's your name?'

'Marie,' said the girl.

'You don't speak Fulfulde, do you, Marie?'

'No,' said the girl. 'I only speak French, Moré and Dula.'

'Where are you from?'

'The capital, Ouagadougou. My father is General Alai Crêpe-Sombo. Perhaps you have heard of him.'

'No,' said Sophie.

'He is making a speech in Gorom-Gorom today to launch his election campaign.'

'That's nice,' said Sophie. 'Now, Marie, are you going to buy a cassette?'

'How much are they?'

'Twelve thousand francs.'

The girl's eyes widened. 'That seems a little expensive.'

'Of course it's expensive,' said Sophie, rolling her eyes. 'Gidaado the Fourth here is the best griot in the province.'

'Oh. Well, in that case...' Marie took a red purse out of her handbag, and began to rifle through a wad of notes. Sophie smiled to herself.

Gidaado had been looking on in bewilderment. Now he leaned towards the girl and handed her a cassette. She looked up at him.

'*Cadeau*,' said Gidaado, grinning from ear to ear.

Cadeau was French for 'present'.

'*Merci beaucoup*,' said Marie and smiled prettily. She put the cassette in her handbag, turned on her heel and left. Gidaado goggled after her.

For a moment Sophie was too angry to speak. 'WHAT THE ZORKI DID YOU DO THAT FOR?' she spluttered at last.

'I felt sorry for her,' said Gidaado.

'YOU felt sorry for HER?'

'She's a stranger here, Sophie. You of all people should know what that feels like.'

'Do you know how much your poor little stranger was about to give you?' said Sophie.

'How much?' asked Gidaado, interested.

'Enough for you to buy your grandmother's medicine and two sacks of millet,' said Sophie, and she pressed the EJECT button so hard that the cassette flew out and landed in the dust on the ground. She put her cassette player under her arm, grabbed her dancing flowers and stomped off.

Two minutes later she was back.

'I thought you didn't speak French,' she said, glaring at Gidaado.

'I don't,' said Gidaado. 'But everyone knows the word *cadeau*, don't they? It's what we used to shout at the tourists when we were little. Sometimes they would give us sweets or biros.'

'Typical,' said Sophie, and stomped off again.

Chapter 9

Sophie lay on her bed and stared up at the gecko on the ceiling above her. It was the middle of the day and she felt unbearably hot and sticky. Flies buzzed tiredly around her room and occasionally bumped into the white mosquito netting over the bed. Up on the top shelf Ali Farka Touré was crooning softly on the cassette player, but the dancing flowers were away in the drawer of Sophie's desk. She did not want to even look at them any more. It had been three days since the Marie incident and Sophie was still feeling bad. The gecko gazed down at her with its lidless eyes and clicked disapprovingly.

How could Gidaado have thrown away his one big business opportunity? After everything she had done to help him. Generosity is one thing, thought Sophie, recklessness is another.

'POLIO VACCINATIONS IN THE MARKETPLACE TOMORROW!' shouted a voice passing along the street outside. It was one of the town criers, but not Gidaado. 'BRING YOUR CHILDREN! FREE OF CHARGE! BRING YOUR CHILDREN! FREE OF CHARGE!'

Sophie turned her face to the wall and thought about Marie's red hair and camel-skin handbag. She remembered the way Gidaado had goggled. He was Sophie's only friend in Gorom-Gorom and she did not want anyone to spoil that. *Is that why I'm angry?* she wondered. *Am I really that selfish?*

'PEOPLE OF GOROM-GOROM!' shouted a voice in the street. Another crier, thought Sophie. Why do they have to make their stupid announcements during siesta time?

'PEOPLE OF GOROM-GOROM! THE OUDALAN PROVINCE CAMEL RACE WILL TAKE PLACE ON MONDAY!'

Sophie sat up. The Oudalan Province Camel Race – hadn't Gidaado once talked about wanting to enter that with Chobbal? Monday was the day after tomorrow!

'ALL ENTRANTS MUST PICK UP A NUMBER-PLATE FROM THE MAYOR'S SECRETARY AT THE TOWN HALL. ANY CAMEL WITHOUT A NUMBER-PLATE WILL BE DISQUALIFIED!'

Amazing! Here was another chance for Gidaado to help his family. Where was he? Out in his village or here in Gorom-Gorom? She must find a way to get the news to him quickly.

'ANY CAMEL CAUGHT CHEWING COLA NUTS OR OTHER PERFORMANCE-ENHANCING DRUGS WILL BE DISQUALIFIED!'

The crier's voice got quieter as he moved off down the street. Sophie listened until the voice was no more than a faint hum in the distance and then she untucked her mosquito net and sprang out of bed. The gecko on the ceiling stared as she slipped her feet into her sandals and dashed out of the room.

'Dad!' Sophie called as she passed the study door. 'I have to go out!'

'Two-thirty,' came a faint voice from within.

Sophie slammed the front door, ran down the path, opened the high metal gate and ran smack into a set of fine strong teeth coming the other way. Camel teeth.

'*Salam alaykum*,' said a familiar voice.

Sophie got up off the ground and brushed herself down. She would have a big bump on her forehead tomorrow morning, but she was pleased to see Gidaado and Chobbal. '*Alaykum asalam*,' she said.

'Are you passing the day in peace?'

'Peace only. How is your grandmother?'

'Peace only. She needs medicine. How are you?'

'Peace only,' said Sophie. 'About the other day, I'm sorry I stomped off like that.'

'That's all right,' said Gidaado. 'I'm sorry I gave away our cassette like that.'

'*Your* cassette,' said Sophie. 'Anyway, you have a second chance. Have you heard the news?'

'The Oudalan Province Camel Race? Of course. I've just come from the town hall.'

'And?'

'And Chobbal will be wearing number 10 on Monday!'

Sophie clapped her hands. 'That's fab!' she said.

'And Sam Saman will be wearing number 3.'

'That's less fab. I didn't even know he had a camel.'

'He does.'

'A fast one?'

'Like lightning. Rumour has it that Saman's father bought it a few years ago from—' Gidaado lowered his voice to a whisper, '*Moussa ag Litni.*'

'*Zorki,*' said Sophie. Moussa ag Litni was a wicked Tuareg bandit who had trained the fastest camels in the whole of West Africa. Ag Litni himself was no longer at large but some of his camels obviously were. 'What do you think?' asked Sophie. 'Can you beat Saman?'

'I have to beat him. Uncle Ibrahiim says that if Chobbal doesn't win the race we must sell him.'

Sophie was shocked. 'Why?'

'There's nothing else to sell,' said Gidaado simply. 'If we do it sooner rather than later we can get a better price for him.'

Sophie said nothing. Tears pricked the back of her eyes.

'Cheer up,' said Gidaado. 'If we win the race, our prize is a big gold nugget and our problems are over, at least for a few months. A gold nugget will buy about fifteen sacks of millet. If we win the race, Chobbal stays with me.'

'Well then,' said Sophie. 'It's clear what you have to do.'

Gidaado nodded gravely. He reached down and stroked Chobbal's tufty white neck. 'Yes,' he said. 'We have to run faster than the harmattan wind.'

Chapter 10

Sophie left the house on Monday morning with a tremendous feeling of excitement. Today would be the four hundred and fourth Oudalan Province Camel Race, but it was Sophie's first, and she cared about the result too much for comfort. She was so nervous that she had not even been able to eat her usual bowl of maize flakes.

The race was to be held on the vast sandy plain beyond the white rock Tondiakara. When Sophie arrived there she found a multitude of villagers and townspeople, gossiping happily in groups. At the centre of one cluster Salif dan

Bari was telling the story of his rope bite and explaining how his rope pills had saved his life. Elsewhere Belko Sambo was showing off his new mobile phone to a group of wide-eyed cattle-herders. Further along, Al Haji Wahib was taking bets on the upcoming camel race.

'The favourite for today's race,' said Al Haji Wahib, 'is Hurryhump at three to one, ridden by reigning champion Mustafa ag Imran. Next up is Fat Wah at five to one, ridden by the exquisitely beautiful Salimata bin Lina. Come and place your bets.'

Sophie went to the starting line. At one end of the line were some wicker chairs on which were seated the mayor of Gorom-Gorom and the chiefs of all the villages in Oudalan. Behind the line fourteen camels paced nervously to and fro. Their riders were sitting bolt upright in their saddles and trying to avoid eye contact with one another. Gidaado was there, wearing a borrowed number 10 football shirt. He was leaning over and murmuring in Chobbal's ear. Sam Saman was sitting in the saddle of a muscular beige camel and smirking across at Gidaado.

'Hey, skink-teeth!' called Saman. 'There you are! You're so thin now that I can hardly see you!'

Gidaado ignored him.

'Nice camel,' yelled Saman. 'What did you say his name was?'

'Chobbal,' said Gidaado quietly.

'Good name,' said Saman, 'because we're going to eat him for breakfast.' He cackled at his own joke and a few of the other riders laughed as well. Gidaado stared straight ahead and tightened his grip on Chobbal's reins.

Gidaado's cousin Hussein appeared next to Sophie, sucking on a stick of sugar cane. They greeted each other and Sophie asked him where his brother Hassan was.

'He's back home in Giriiji with Uncle Ibrahiim,' said Hussein. 'They are practising a praise-song for whoever wins the race today.'

'Why aren't you with them?'

'I am just the calabash player, aren't I? Besides, I need to go and let them know who has won, so they can make the last-minute changes.'

The hubbub of the crowd was suddenly drowned out by a voice so loud that the sand vibrated underneath Sophie's feet. She looked up with a start to see a small bearded man standing on top of Tondiakara. He wore a red beret and very dark glasses. Sophie recognized him as Furki Baa Turki, the loudest crier in Oudalan.

'PEOPLE OF GOROM-GOROM!' cried the man, hopping from foot to foot. 'Welcome to the four hundred and fourth OUDALAN PROVINCE CAMEL RACE!'

'Isn't he brilliant?' laughed Hussein, putting his fingers in his ears.

'PLEASE UNDERSTAND,' yelled Furki Baa Turki, 'that the Oudalan Province Camel Race has a STRICT no-biting policy, which applies to all contestants and their camels. Other rules are as follows: NO leaping from one camel to another, NO grabbing of ears or tails, NO unsheathing of swords. NO swearing in Fulfulde, French, Tamasheq, Songhai, Bambara, Moré, Dula or Arabic, except for the word "*Zorki*" which each contestant may say up to three times. Contestants will run to the Sheik Amadou calabash tree, go round it ONCE and return to this point. The FIRST camel to cross the line will be declared the winner, so long as it has on its saddle the SAME rider who started the race on it. The judges' decision is final. NO attacking the judges after the race. NO strangling the winner, NO stealing his or her gold nugget, and NO declarations of war on his or her village. IS THAT CLEAR?'

'YES,' cried the fourteen riders in their various languages, tiptoeing their camels up to the starting line.

'Good,' said Furki Baa Turki. 'It is a GREAT HONOUR for me to introduce the celebrity who will start today's race. He came all the way from OUAGADOUGOU yesterday on a VERY bumpy dirt track, VOMITING all the way, and last night he didn't get a WINK of sleep on account of the DONKEYS, ROOSTERS and WILD DOGS just outside his window. Please welcome MONSIEUR ISAAKU SAODOGO, the Chief Assistant of the Assistant Chief at the *OUAGADOUGOU INSTITUTE OF TOPO-GRAPHY AND CADASTRAL PLANNING*!!!'

The crowd went wild. A small man in a neat white suit stepped up onto Tondiakara next to Furki Baa Turki. He had bags under his eyes and he kept sneezing.

'Monsieur Saodogo has a severe CAMEL ALLERGY and an even more severe DUST ALLERGY, yet he has honoured us with his presence here today!'

The crowd clapped and stamped their

appreciation, sending great clouds of red dust billowing into the air. The man in white wheezed and sneezed and clutched his collar.

'Monsieur Saodogo was signalling to me a moment ago that he has COMPLETELY lost his voice, so we will forego the speeches and let him go ahead and start the race. THE FOUR HUNDRED AND FOURTH OUDALAN PROVINCE CAMEL RACE WILL START AT THE MOMENT THAT MONSIEUR SAODOGO NEXT SNEEZES!!!!'

There was rapturous applause from the crowd and then some urgent *shush*-ing and then silence. Everyone's attention was concentrated on the figure in white. He was bent over double, struggling to undo the top button of his collar. His eyes were streaming and his nose twitched.

A Tuareg rider adjusted his copious turban. Saman's camel lowered its head and snorted. Gidaado fingered Chobbal's reins and stared in front of him, as unblinking as a gecko.

'A-TCHOO,' said Monsieur Saodogo.

'HOOSH-KA!' cried fourteen voices, and the camels sped off, their hooves pounding the sand.

Chapter 11

'HOOSH-BARAKAAAA!' cried the camel riders, getting into top gear as soon as possible.

For the first fifty metres of the race the camels galloped along in a pack and it was difficult to tell who was in the lead. Then one of the Tuareg riders nosed in front, his copious white turban flapping in the wind. His camel had a fine leather saddle edged with silver and gold.

'That's Mustafa ag Imran,' said Hussein. 'He's fast and he's tricky so watch out for him. He won this race last year.'

Sophie looked for Chobbal and saw him streaking along in fifth place. *Go on, Chobbal*, she breathed. *Run your heart out.*

In second place now was a tall light-skinned woman whose long black hair streamed out behind her, shining in the sun. She was rocking back and forth gracefully in time with her camel's strides. Sophie had seen her at the starting line and had noticed that her lips were tattooed black in striking contrast with her light skin. Amongst Fulani women tattooed lips were considered beautiful.

'Salimata bin Lina,' said Hussein devoutly. 'Look at her go.'

In third place was Saman, leaning right forward in his saddle. He was twirling an acacia branch in his hand and bringing it down on his camel's side with sharp cracks. Each time the camel felt the whip it sprang forward in terror. It was cruel but it was working. Bit by bit, Saman was drawing level with bin Lina.

Mustafa ag Imran reached the calabash tree first, and as he went round it he grabbed hold of a long bendy branch. He bent the branch forward until it could go no further, then ducked under it and let it go. The branch flew backwards.

Sam Saman saw the branch just in time and he ducked hurriedly. Riding beside him, Salimata bin Lina was less quick. The branch hit her with a sickening *thwack* just above her beautiful tattooed lips, knocking her clean off her camel.

'*Oooh!*' said the crowd.

Mustafa ag Imran glanced back and let out an evil guttural laugh, muffled slightly by the folds of his turban.

'Is that allowed?' said Sophie, turning to Hussein.

'You tell me,' said Hussein. 'Did you hear anything in the rules about not touching the calabash tree?'

'No,' said Sophie.

'Then it's allowed. It's a superb piece of strategic racing.'

The racers galloped on. Mustafa ag Imran was still in first place, Sam Saman in second. Gidaado was back in third place, just rounding the calabash tree.

'*COME ON, GIDAADO!*' yelled Sophie. '*STAY WITH THEM!*'

Saman's camel was gaining ground on the Tuareg with every stride. Camels trained by the famous bandit Moussa ag Litni were known for their stamina, and the second half of the race was sure to be good for this one. Whipping his camel savagely, Saman came up on the outside of Mustafa ag Imran until he was within arm's reach of him. He leaned over and grabbed the flapping end of the Tuareg's turban.

'*Zorki,*' came the muffled voice of Mustafa ag Imran.

Saman yanked the turban hard, pulling the Tuareg half out of his saddle.

'*Zorki!*' said ag Imran.

'*Bahaat-ugh!*' cried Saman, and his camel screeched to a halt. As the Tuareg's camel ran on, Saman held onto the turban with both hands. Sophie cringed. Mustafa ag Imran spun round twice, flew off his camel backwards and landed in the dust.

'*Oooh!*' said the crowd, and there was the unmistakeable sound of lots of people tearing up their betting slips.

'*Hoosh-ka!*' cried Saman, and his camel sprinted off again.

'That's terrible,' said Sophie. '*Surely* Saman will be disqualified for that.'

'Grabbing of ears or tails is forbidden,' said

Hussein, 'but there is nothing in the rules about yanking turbans. It is a superb piece of strategic racing.'

Saman's brief stop was of course just what Gidaado needed. He was not far off the lead now and the gap was closing fast.

'*COME ON, GIDAADO!*' shouted Sophie, jumping up and down. '*YOU CAN DO IT!*'

There were about a hundred metres left of the race. Gidaado crouched low in his saddle and his borrowed number 10 shirt billowed in the wind. Chobbal was a blur of white, moving faster than Sophie had ever seen him go.

Saman glanced back and looked amazed to see Chobbal right on his tail. He put his hand in his pocket and drew it out again, closed into a tight fist. *What have you got there?* thought Sophie.

With eighty metres to go, Gidaado was right up alongside his rival, their camels so close that their flanks were touching. Sophie could see the look of concentration on Gidaado's face as he tried to nose Chobbal in front. Saman lifted his whip and brought it down hard on Gidaado's back.

'*Oooh!*' said the crowd.

Sophie yelped as if she and not Gidaado had been hit. 'SURELY that's not allowed!' she cried.

'There is nothing in the rules about whipping your opponent,' said Hussein. 'In fact, it is a superb piece of strategic ra—'

'It is NOT!' shouted Sophie. 'That's your COUSIN being whipped out there!'

Again and again Saman's acacia whip came down across Gidaado's back. Gidaado flinched each time but he stayed firmly in the saddle and kept his eyes straight ahead. It would take more than a whipping to make him lose this race.

Sophie put her hands over her eyes and peeked through her fingers, hardly daring to watch. Chobbal's nose was slightly in front. Now his whole head was in front. Now his whole head and neck. With fifty metres to go, even his hump was in front. *He's going to win*, thought Sophie, hardly daring to believe it. *Chobbal is going to win.*

Gidaado was almost a whole camel's length ahead of Sam Saman. With an audible snarl Saman reached across towards Chobbal's tail. *If he grabs the tail, he is disqualified*, thought Sophie happily. But Saman did not grab the tail. He drew back his hand and took hold of the reins of his own camel once more. *He's given up*, thought Sophie. *Sam Saman has given up!*

Chobbal was out in front and running well. Sophie could see the whites of Gidaado's eyes and the perspiration on his brow. He was grinning in triumph, knowing that the race was his. *He's almost won*, thought Sophie. *Chobbal has almost won! Gidaado won't have to sell him. The people of Giriiji will be able to buy millet. Gidaado's grandmother will get her medicine.*

Then it happened. Chobbal's snowy flank shuddered. The muscles in his neck convulsed and his eyes rolled. He started to stumble.

'*Oooh*,' cried the crowd.

Chobbal staggered a few more strides before his legs buckled underneath him. He crashed to the ground less than ten metres from the finish line and Gidaado rolled off his back into the dust. Boy and camel lay there side by side, not moving.

Saman charged past them and crossed the line. The crowd clapped and cheered and surged forward, flocking around Saman's winning camel and the bodies of Gidaado and Chobbal.

'WE HAVE A WINNER!' cried Furki Baa Turki. 'NUMBER 3, SAM SAMAN, HAS WON THE FOUR HUNDRED AND FOURTH OUDALAN PROVINCE CAMEL RACE!!!!!!!!'

'No!' cried Sophie and she began to push her way through the mob.

'The boy is okay,' said a woman's voice. 'He's already beginning to come round.'

Sophie reached the front of the crowd. Chobbal was lying on the ground perfectly still, and a tall thin man was bending over him. *Where have I seen that man before?* thought Sophie.

'What's the matter?' she cried, throwing herself down beside the stricken camel and stroking his ears. 'Why did he collapse?'

The tall man straightened up and put something red in his pocket.

'It is not serious,' he said. 'A build up of lactic acid, nothing more.'

Sophie stared at him blankly.

'A stitch,' said the man. 'The camel got a stitch from all that running.'

'Rubbish!' cried Sophie, and all around her the crowd drew in their breath sharply. 'Having a stitch hurts but it doesn't make you collapse.'

'Is that right?' said the man, his eyes flashing. 'I suppose you have a university degree in camel biology, do you? Have you ever *seen* a camel with a stitch?'

It was then that Sophie recognized him.

'No, I haven't,' she said, standing up slowly. 'But at the market the other week I did see a bull knocked out by a sleep dart.'

A muscle twitched in the tall man's face, but he said nothing.

Gidaado was sitting up now and shaking his head from side to side. Sam Saman stepped through the crowd and stood over him.

'Good race,' he said, smiling down at Gidaado. 'Are you coming to the award ceremony? I believe my prize is a rather large gold nugget.'

Sophie walked towards him, her heart pounding.

'How much did it cost, Saman?' she said, trying to keep her voice from shaking.

'What?' said Saman.

'The sleep dart. How much did you pay this man for it?'

Saman laughed. '*Zorki*, Gidaado,' he said. 'What is the matter with your white girlfriend? I think a djinn has jumped on her head and sent her a bit bonkers.'

Blood rushed to Sophie's face. She clenched her fists and advanced on Saman. The mob pressed in around them, hoping for a good scrap.

Sophie felt a hand on her shoulder and she turned to see Hussein standing behind her.

'Leave it, Sophie,' said Hussein. 'There's nothing in the rules about sleep darts.'

'That's all right, then, isn't it?' said Sophie. 'I suppose YOU thought that shoving that dart into Chobbal's backside was A SUPERB PIECE OF STRATEGIC RACING?'

'No,' said Hussein.

'Good,' said Sophie. 'Because if you did, I would buy one for *YOUR* backside.'

With that, she turned and pushed her way through the crowd and walked away as fast as she could, Saman's laughter ringing in her ears.

Chapter 12

On market day, Gidaado did not come to
Sophie's house. She went to the animal market
and found him there, standing with Chobbal not
far from the other camel-sellers. She was
surprised at how peaceful Gidaado seemed.

'Aren't you angry?' she asked.

'A bit,' he said. 'But there is nothing I can do
now, is there?'

'You could strangle Saman, for a start,' said
Sophie. 'Look, he's coming this way.'

'No,' said Gidaado quietly. 'Strangling the
winner is forbidden in the rules of the race.

Besides, he's bigger than me.'

'I warn you,' said Sophie, flexing her fingers. 'If you won't do it, I will.'

Sam Saman strolled up to them. He was wearing a pair of shiny new shoes and eating a banana.

'*Salam alaykum*,' said Saman.

'*Alaykum asalam*,' said Gidaado.

'Selling the camel?'

'Yes.'

'Times are hard, are they?'

'Yes.'

'I'll do you a favour,' said Saman. 'Give me the albino camel and I'll give you the rest of this banana.'

Sophie opened her mouth to say something, but her attention was caught by a Land Rover zooming in through the gates of the animal market. What was going on? Usually vehicles were not allowed in amongst the animals.

The Land Rover circled a few times and then came and stopped right in front of them. The passenger door opened and a man in army uniform stepped out.

Then the back doors opened and two more people got out. One of them was a giant of a man dressed in black. The other was a red-haired girl carrying a camel-skin handbag. Sophie groaned inwardly as she recognized Marie.

'*Bon soir*,' said the uniformed man, holding out a large hand to Gidaado. 'They told me I would find you here.'

'*Alaykum asalam*,' said Gidaado, shaking the hand and gawping at the medals on the man's uniform. They were mounted neatly on three strips of leather and they gleamed in the dazzling midday sun.

'Is this him?' said the man in French.

Marie nodded.

'And this is his translator?'

'Yes,' said Marie.

'What is your name, translator-girl?' said the man, holding out his hand to Sophie.

'Sophie,' she said, taking it.

'I am General Alai Crêpe-Sombo,' said the man. 'You have already met my daughter.'

'Yes,' said Sophie.

'And this is Pougini, my bodyguard,' said the General.

Sophie glanced at the giant and noticed a mean-looking truncheon in his belt.

'Sophie,' said General Crêpe-Sombo, 'tell

your friend that I have been listening to his cassette all week. Marie here plays it so loudly in her room that everyone in the house is forced to listen to it.'

Sophie translated the General's words into Fulfulde and Gidaado's eyes widened.

'Has he come to murder me?' he said.

'Let's hope so,' said Saman, admiring the giant's truncheon. Saman did not understand French, but he was listening in on Sophie's translations with great interest.

'Usually,' continued the General, 'I am not a fan of my daughter's music. She is fond of *le rap*, a sound which I detest more than the taunts of an enemy army on the far bank of a fast-flowing river.'

Sophie translated and Gidaado nodded sympathetically.

'But *you*,' said the General, poking Gidaado in the chest, '*you* I like.'

When Sophie translated, Gidaado puffed out his cheeks with relief.

'I may not understand Fulfulde,' said the General, 'but I can tell a good griot when I hear one. And my daughter tells me that you are the best griot in Oudalan province.'

Sophie translated. Gidaado grinned modestly and shot an adoring glance at the General's daughter.

'No, he's not!' cried Saman, stepping forward. 'He's not even a proper griot any more. He's just a crier messing about with a *hoddu*.'

'What is this boy saying?' asked the General.

'I'd rather not translate that if you don't mind,' said Sophie. 'It was not very polite.'

The General glared at Saman and then continued. 'Last week,' he said, 'I launched my election campaign to become President of this country. I have great support in Ouagadougou and in the south, but I also need people here in the north to vote for me. People must understand that *I* am the man who will solve all their problems and give them hope for the future.'

Sophie translated for Gidaado and he nodded enthusiastically as if he really believed it.

'In the old days,' said General Crêpe-Sombo, 'a man who wanted to become chief would hire a griot to be his praise-singer. The griot would follow that man wherever he went and sing about what a fine fellow he was. What *I* need for my Gorom-Gorom campaign is a griot like that.'

As Sophie translated the General's words into Fulfulde, she suddenly understood what this was all about. General Crêpe-Sombo was about to offer Gidaado a job as a praise-singer, the highest honour for any griot. And all because of that daft cassette they had recorded together.

Saman had also understood. 'Choose me, choose me!' he cried, hopping from foot to foot and waving his hands in the General's face. 'I am a griot. I sing, I play the *hoddu*, I dance. I was born in this town, I know everyone here. I won the camel race. People here like me. People will listen to me. If you choose me, you can't *not* win the election.'

The General stared at him in bewilderment.

'What is this impudent boy trying to say to me?' he asked.

Sophie looked down and shuffled her feet in the sand. 'I would rather not translate it,' she said.

'I *order* you to tell me,' said the General. 'What did the boy say to me?'

'All right,' said Sophie, 'but I want you to know that Gidaado and I do *not* agree with the things he said.'

'*Tell me*,' said the General, breathing heavily through his nose.

Sophie sighed deeply and said in her best French, 'Go home. Go home. You smell like a dead skink. Your medals are probably stolen. Get out of our town and take your camel-faced daughter with you. No one here likes you. No one will listen to you. Crawl back into your hole, you can't possibly win the election.'

The General's mouth dropped open and his eyes bulged. He gave a roar of anger and turned to his bodyguard.

'POUGINI,' he bellowed. 'SEIZE this impudent boy and do to him what you did to Lieutenant Aladad last Thursday.'

The giant pulled the truncheon out of his belt and advanced on Saman.

'What's the matter?' cried Saman. 'What are you doing?'

'He says you don't scare him,' said Sophie sweetly. 'He says you're a brainless baboon.'

The bodyguard roared and reached out to grab Saman.

Saman did not wait to be grabbed. He dodged the giant's outstretched hand and scampered away as fast as a meerkat, shrieking as he went. The bodyguard dashed after him, waving his truncheon in the air and yelling horrible threats in French, including many words that Sophie had not learned in class.

'Back to business,' said the General briskly. 'Monsieur Gidaado, I want you to be my praise-singer for the next six months. I want you to sing songs and dance dances and speak speeches that will make people love me. Do you think you can do that?'

Sophie turned to Gidaado. 'Do you want to work for this man?' she asked him in Fulfulde.

'Are you crazy?' said Gidaado. 'Of course I do!'

'He says it depends,' said Sophie in French, turning back to the General. 'He wants to know how much you're offering him.'

'Twenty thousand a month,' said the General.

'He says he'll give you twenty thousand francs a month,' said Sophie to Gidaado.

'You must be joking!' cried Gidaado. 'That's wonderful!'

'He says you must be joking,' said Sophie to the General. 'He wants at least fifty.'

'Thirty-five,' said the General.

'The General would like to raise that to thirty-five thousand a month,' said Sophie.

'*Zorki*,' said Gidaado.

'He says forty,' said Sophie to the General.

The General stared at Gidaado and sighed. 'Monsieur Gidaado drives a hard bargain,' he said, 'but I accept. Forty thousand a month for six months, plus two Alai Crêpe-Sombo T-shirts. Deal or no deal?'

Sophie smiled at the General. 'Deal,' she said.

The shadows of day lengthened and faded and the sun turned crimson. Sophie and Gidaado were sitting on the gravel outside Sophie's house, shelling peanuts and listening to 'Greatest Hits of Ali Farka Touré'. Behind them Chobbal munched guiltily on Sophie's dad's sunflowers.

'Forty thousand a month for six months,' Gidaado was saying. 'It's enough for the whole village to live on. Wait until Uncle Ibrahiim hears about this.'

'You don't think he'll still want to sell Chobbal?' said Sophie.

'Sell Chobbal? No way. He'll be kissing Chobbal!'

Sophie laughed. Considering what a depressing month it had been, things were turning out rather well. Gidaado and his family would not go hungry. His grandmother would get her medicine. And with Gidaado in General Crêpe-Sombo's service, Sam Saman was sure to steer clear of them all for a very long time indeed.

Sophie changed the cassette and the soulful intro of 'Mucky Tail I miss you' soared over the thatched rooftops of Gorom-Gorom. A red-necked lizard scuttled up to them and bobbed up and down, looking for all the world as if it was dancing.

'Your days as a cow-crier are over now,' said Sophie. 'You must be ecstatic.'

'Not at all,' said Gidaado. 'Being a crier was great. I wish you would stop dissing it.'

Sophie threw a handful of peanut shells over him, and he cackled.

'Gidaado,' said Sophie. 'You remember that thing you said about Joy? How it's like drops of milk splashing out of a calabash and wetting your face and arms?'

'I remember,' said Gidaado. 'But you said you don't know what that feels like.'

Sophie grinned. 'I'm beginning to,' she said.